MERMAID DAYS™

A New Friend

Read more MERMAID DAYS™ books!

MERMAID DAYS™

The Sunken Ship

ACORN™

WRITTEN BY
Kyle Lukoff

ART BY
Kat Uno

SCHOLASTIC

MERMAID DAYS

The Sea Monster

ACORN™

WRITTEN BY
Kyle Lukoff

ART BY
Kat Uno

SCHOLASTIC

MERMAID DAYS™

A
New
Friend

WRITTEN BY
Kyle Lukoff

ART BY
Kat Uno

🌱 ACORN™
SCHOLASTIC INC.

For Olympia Bruce
—**KL**

Thank you to all the little readers who I hope enjoy this book!
—**KU**

Library of Congress Cataloging-in-Publication Data

Names: Lukoff, Kyle, author. | Uno, Kat, illustrator.
Title: A new friend / written by Kyle Lukoff; art by Kat Uno.
Description: First edition. | New York : Acorn/Scholastic Inc., 2023. |
Series: Mermaid days; 3 | Audience: Ages 4–6. | Audience: Grades K–1. |
Summary: When mermaid Vera and Octo-boy Beaker investigate what seems like a wave of vandalism in Tidal Grove, they discover a baby Mantis shrimp who does not fully understand his own power, and help him find his family.
Identifiers: LCCN 2022021157 | ISBN 9781338794977 (paperback) |
ISBN 9781338794984 (library binding)
Subjects: LCSH: Mermaids—Juvenile fiction. | Marine animals—Juvenile fiction. | Friendship—Juvenile fiction. | CYAC: Mermaids—Fiction. |
Marine animals—Fiction. | Friendship—Fiction. | BISAC: JUVENILE FICTION / Readers / Beginner | JUVENILE FICTION / Mermaids & Mermen | LCGFT: Picture books.
Classification: LCC PZ7.1.L8456 Ne 2023 | DDC [E]—dc23
LC record available at https://lccn.loc.gov/2022021157

10 9 8 7 6 5 4 3 2 1   23 24 25 26 27

Printed in China   62
First edition, September 2023
Edited by Rachel Matson
Designed by Jaime Lucero

TABLE OF CONTENTS

WHO LIVES IN TIDAL GROVE?

Vera

Beaker

Beaker's Legs

Mr. Burbles

Kelpie

Baby Mantis Shrimp

LOST AND FOUND

My library books are due today. I better take them back!

THE NEW SQUID

THE LITTLE HUMAN

MARY ANNA'S TRENCH

Oh no! Come back, books!

4

6

7

That shell is smashed, too.

And there's a hole in that fence.

It's a trail of broken things! Let's follow it.

That is a mantis shrimp. And that blast is why I said to be careful! They have cool powers.

Wow! Thanks for saving us from that shark.

I guess this tiny shrimp broke all those things in town.

DID YOU KNOW?

Mantis shrimp are very small. But they can make themselves look much bigger.

They are also very strong! They punch water to create shock waves. Some shock waves are strong enough to break glass.

LIBRARIAN

It is a bad idea to get into a fight with a mantis shrimp!

Mantis shrimp usually grow to be about four inches long.

Mantis shrimp can make themselves look really big.

blast!

Mantis shrimp can punch water to create shock waves!

19

FINDING FAMILY

This baby mantis shrimp is lost! I wonder where it came from.

I bet its family is looking for it! Let's help.

21

I have never seen a mantis shrimp before. Where do you think its family is?

I bet we can find them! Look, the side of the sunken ship is smashed.

Look at that glass bottle! It's broken, too.

Let's go that way!

I see a tunnel of torn seaweed!

28

Whew! I'm dizzy.

Getting blasted was fun, though.

That was rude.

We were just trying to help.

33

Did they think we were going to hurt them?

Probably! We are much bigger than they are.

34

THE BOX

Vera, come look at this!
A box fell off a boat.

I love when that happens.
Remember when we found
a box of bicycles?

I couldn't ride one at all!

41

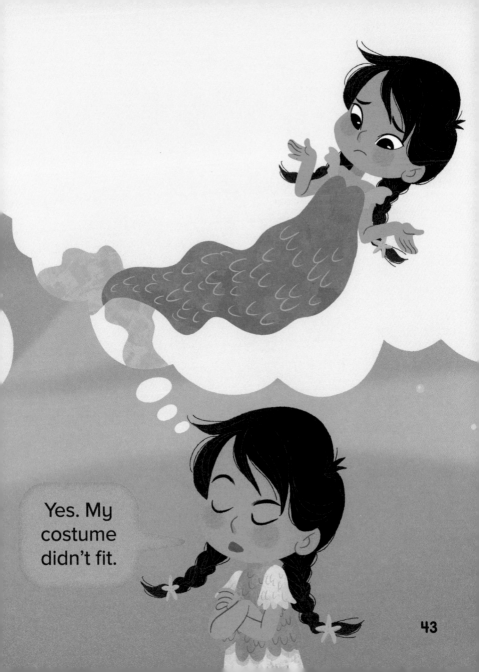

Yes. My costume didn't fit.

43

You pull that way!

You push this way!

I'll get this corner.

Be careful!

I hope there's food inside.

45

Hi, baby mantis shrimp! We found this box. And we want to know what's inside.

But we can't open it! Can you help us?

47

49

plink

plink

52

53

ABOUT THE CREATORS

KYLE LUKOFF has never met a mermaid. He would very much like to be friends with an octopus! But he would rather climb trees than go to the beach, and he would rather write books for kids than learn how to scuba dive. He is a National Book Award finalist and the Newbery and Stonewall award–winning author of lots of books, including WHEN AIDAN BECAME A BROTHER and TOO BRIGHT TO SEE.

KAT UNO was born, raised, and currently resides in Hawaii. Living on an island surrounded by the beautiful Pacific Ocean has always provided much inspiration. Kat has loved being creative ever since she was little. She enjoys illustrating children's books, and mermaids are one of her favorite subjects to draw! She is also a proud mom of two eager readers.

YOU CAN DRAW BEAKER!

1 Draw the outline of Beaker's head, torso, and lower body.

2 Add eight wiggly legs to their lower body.

3 Add short sleeves on their shirt and give the two arms and hands.

4 Draw their hair. Then give them an ear.

5 Draw Beaker's face and add details to their legs.

6 Color in your drawing!

WHAT'S YOUR STORY?

Vera and Beaker meet a baby mantis shrimp.
Imagine that **you** meet a baby mantis shrimp!
What game would you like to play?
How would you play together?
Write and draw your story!